This book
belongs to

_____

_____

For my little, big sister
Joyce Dunbar

For all factory farm animals,
that one day they will be as free
as the animals in Eggday.

Jane Cabrera

This edition first published in 2007 by Alligator Books Ltd.

cupcake

Cupcake is an imprint of Alligator Books Ltd.
Gadd House, Arcadia Avenue, London N3 2JU

Text © Joyce Dunbar 1999
Illustrations © Jane Cabrera 1999

1 3 5 7 9 10 8 6 4 2

The right of Joyce Dunbar and Jane Cabrera to be identified as the author
and illustrator of this work has been asserted by them in accordance with
the Copyright, Designs and Patents Act, 1988.
A CIP record for this title is available from the British Library.

ISBN: 978-1-84750-180-6

Printed in Malaysia

Eggday

Joyce Dunbar Illustrated by Jane Cabrera

cupcake

Dora, the duck, said to Pogson, the pig, "Tomorrow is Eggday

"What's Eggday?" asked Pogson.

"We are having a best egg competition," said Dora.

"But what can I bring?" asked Pogson.
"A pig egg," said Dora, and she
waddled over to tell Humphrey, the horse.

"Tomorrow is Eggday," said Dora.

"What's Eggday?" asked Humphrey.

"We are having a best egg competition," said Dora.

"But what can I bring?" said Humphrey.

"A horse egg," said Dora, and she waddled over to tell Gideon, the goat.

"Tomorrow is Eggday," said Dora.

"What's Eggday?" asked Gideon.

"We are having a best egg competition," said Dora.

"But what can I bring?" asked Gideon.

"A goat egg," said Dora, and she waddled back to her nest.

"Where will I get a pig egg? Pogson, the pig, asked Humphrey, the horse.

"Where will I get a horse egg?"
Humphrey, the horse, asked
Gideon, the goat.

"Where will I get a goat egg?"
Gideon, the goat, asked himself.

Hetty Hen came to see what the matter was.

"What's all the fuss?" she asked.

"It's **Eggday** tomorrow," said Pogson, "I am trying to lay a pig egg."

"But pigs don't lay eggs," said Hetty. "Pigs have piglets. And you're not even a sow."

"And I am trying to lay a horse egg," said Humphrey.

"But horses don't lay eggs," said Hetty. "Horses have foals. And you're not even a mare."

"And I am trying to lay a goat egg," said Gideon.

"But goats don't lay eggs," said Hetty. "Goats have kids. And you're a billy goat, not a nanny goat."

"But Dora says it's Eggday tomorrow," said Pogson.

"What's Eggday?" asked Hetty.

"We are having a best egg competition,"
said Pogson, "and we all have to take an egg."
"Wait here a moment," said Hetty,
"and I'll see what I can find in my coop."

Hetty came back with three eggs.
"Here's one for you," she said to Pogson.
"Give it a short curly tail and it will look like a pig egg."
"Here's one for you, Humphrey," said Hetty. "Give it a hairy brown mane and it will look like a horse egg."
"What about me?" said Gideon.
"Here's one for you, Gideon. Give it a curved pair of horns and it will look like a goat egg," said Hetty.

So they all went away with their eggs.

In the morning, they met up again. Hetty was last to arrive. "Happy Eggday!" they said to one another, proudly showing off their eggs.

Hetty seemed the proudest of all as she showed them a beautiful, smooth, speckled egg. "I laid this especially!" she clucked.

"Where's Dora?"

"Let's go and find Dora," said Humphrey. And they went along to the hayloft where Dora had made her nest. "Dora! Dora!" called Pogson. "It's **Eggday** today! Come and see my pig egg. My pig egg has a short curly tail."

"And my horse egg has a hairy brown mane!" called Humphrey.

"And my goat egg has a curved pair of horns!" called Gideon.

"And my hen egg is smooth with brown speckles!" called Hetty.

There was silence for a
while, then Dora started to quack. . .
"I've changed my mind," said Dora.
"It isn't Eggday anymore."
"Well, what day is it?"
asked Pogson.

"IT'S DUCKLING DAY!"
Dora quacked proudly.
And she lifted up her wing so that the
animals could peep underneath.

Well – you can guess who
had the best duckling!